My fourth
Enid Blyton book

By the same author

In this series
My first Enid Blyton book
My second Enid Blyton book
My third Enid Blyton book

Also available for younger readers

The Boy Who Turned into an Engine
The Book of Naughty Children
A Second Book of Naughty Children
Ten-Minute Tales
Fifteen-Minute Tales
Twenty-Minute Tales
More Twenty-Minute Tales
The Land of Far-Beyond
Billy-Bob Tales
Tales of Betsy May
Eight O'Clock Tales
The Yellow Story Book
The Red Story Book
The Blue Story Book
The Green Story Book
Tricky the Goblin
The Adventures of Binkle and Flip
Mr Pink-Whistle's Party
Merry Mr Meddle
Mr Meddle's Mischief
Don't Be Silly Mr Twiddle
Adventures of the Wishing Chair
More Adventures of the Wishing Chair
Rag Tag and Bobtail
Tales from the Bible
Children's Life of Christ
Bedtime Stories and Prayers

Enid Blyton

My fourth
Enid Blyton book

DRAGON
Granada Publishing

Dragon Books
Granada Publishing Ltd
8 Grafton Street, London W1X 3LA

Published by Dragon Books 1983
Reprinted 1984

First published in Great Britain by
Latimer House Limited 1955

Copyright © Darrell Waters Ltd 1955

ISBN 0-583-30654-3

Printed and bound in Great Britain by
Collins, Glasgow

Set in Times

Contents

The stories in this book and in My first Enid
Blyton book, My second Enid Blyton book *and*
My third Enid Blyton book, *were first published
in three books, titled* My First Enid Blyton Book,
My Second Enid Blyton Book *and* My Third
Enid Blyton Book *by Latimer House Limited, in
1952, 1953 and 1955 respectively.*

Mr Put-Em-Right

THERE was once a boy whose name was Robert, but he was always called Bossy. It was a very good name for him too, because he was always trying to boss the other children, and put them right, and tell them to do things this way and not that way.

Bossy was a big boy for his age, bigger than the others. It wasn't easy to stand up to him, and nobody dared to call him Bossy to his face. So they had to put up with him – but how he did spoil their games!

'We won't play this game – we'll play another game!' he would say, as soon as he came up. 'I'll be the chief. Harry, you can go over there. Jack, you go over there. Now, you listen to me and I'll tell you exactly what to do.'

Bossy liked to tell the others what to spend their money on too, when they had any. 'No, don't get peppermints,' he would say. 'Get toffee to-day. It's nicer.'

'But I want peppermints,' Jack would say.

'Well, you just buy toffee to-day, and you'll

see I'm right,' Bossy would tell him. And he would march poor Jack off to the sweet-shop and see that he bought toffee. Bossy liked toffee very much – much better than peppermints.

Another thing that the children didn't like about Bossy was the way he found fault with them. 'Your dress is torn,' he would say to Jane. 'You'd better go home and get it mended.' Or he would tell Katy to stop singing. 'I don't like your voice,' he would say, putting his hands over his ears. 'Do stop. You are out of tune!'

So, altogether, Bossy was not very much liked, but because he was so big and so loud-voiced and so determined to have his own way, the other children found it very difficult to go against him.

Now, one day Mr Put-Em-Right's garden-boy fell ill. Mr Put-Em-Right lived in a small cottage at the end of the village, and nobody knew very much about him. They knew he was a sharp-eyed little man, who kept his cottage and garden beautifully, and paid his bills every week, but they didn't know anything else about him.

Well, when his garden-boy fell ill, Mr Put-Em-Right pinned a notice on his gate.

'Wanted. Garden-boy for One Week. Good Wages.'

It was holiday time. The bigger boys looked at the notice, and thought it would be a good

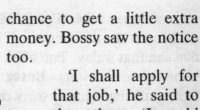

chance to get a little extra money. Bossy saw the notice too.

'I shall apply for that job,' he said to the others. 'I could do with some extra money. I want a new bell for my bicycle and a new pump too. I've heard that Mr Put-Em-Right pays very well.'

'I thought I'd apply for the job, too,' said Jack, and Harry said the same.

'You're smaller than I am,' said Bossy, and he threw out his chest and stood on tiptoe. 'See how big I am. I'm strong too. I bet I could do the garden-work easily – far better than you could.'

'Well, I'm going after the job now,' said Jack, but Bossy pushed him back. 'No, you're not. I'm going first.' And off he went to Mr Put-Em-Right's cottage.

Well, Bossy certainly seemed a big, strong

sort of lad, so Mr Put-Em-Right told him he could start the next morning. He would give him five shillings a day. The work was not hard. The hours were not long. Bossy went home in delight – all that money for work he often had to do for nothing in his father's garden! Marvellous!

He went off the next morning on his bicycle. He met Jack and Harry and they scowled at him. As usual, Bossy had got in first and got what he wanted! Bossy waved to them and shouted cheerfully.

He put his bicycle by the back door. Mr Put-Em-Right came out and looked at him. 'Good morning,' said Bossy.

'Say "Good morning, Mr Put-Em-Right!" or "Good morning, *sir*",' said the old man. 'Good gracious me, your face is dirty. Didn't you wash it this morning? Go and wash under the tap. And smooth your hair down, too, it's sticking up in a very silly manner.'

Bossy opened his mouth to say that he must have got his face dirty on the way there and the wind had blown his hair untidy, but Mr Put-Em-Right silenced him at once.

'No sauce now, not a word from you, understand?'

Bossy washed his face and did his hair. He went out to find Mr Put-Em-Right looking at his bicycle. 'Look here, my boy,' said the old man, pointing a disgusted finger at the bicycle, 'is that the way to keep a nice bike? Look at the dirty wheels! Now, don't answer me back; but you see that you get a rag this evening as soon as you've finished your work, and clean that bicycle properly before you go home.'

Bossy went red. He wasn't used to being ticked off like this, and not being allowed to say a word himself. Mr Put-Em-Right showed him the tool-shed. 'Now there are the tools,' he said. 'I want those peas over there in the garden well-sticked to-day. I want the strawberry bed weeded. I want those lettuces thinned out properly. I want the grass cut. You'll find all the tools here. Now get on with your work.'

Well, Bossy got out the lawn-mower first, and began to cut the grass. But in a minute or two the old man was out again. 'For goodness' sake, don't go round and round the lawn like that, go straight up and down!'

'I don't see that it matters,' said Bossy in surprise. 'This is the way I always do it at home.'

'You're going to do it my way,' said Mr Put-Em-Right firmly. 'I know best. My way is always best. You do as I tell you.'

It was the same with the peas. Bossy felt that he really couldn't go wrong with the peas. It was easy to stick peas. But no. Out came Mr Put-

Em-Right, pulled up all the sticks he had put in, and scolded him for being silly.

'Put *two* rows of sticks, not one,' he said. 'Doesn't a boy like you know anything at all? Here you are, sticking the stakes into the roots of the peas and killing them; put a row on each side of the peas!'

'But,' said Bossy, and that was as far as he got.

'I don't want to hear any buts,' said the old man. 'You think you know everything. You're the stupidest boy I've ever come across. Do as you're told! My goodness, look where your big feet are treading – all on those young turnips. Come off at once! Why didn't you wear boots to garden in instead of those silly shoes? You must wear boots to-morrow.'

'They're not mended,' said Bossy.

'Well, you'll have five shillings to-night if you work a bit better than you have done so far,' said Mr Put-Em-Right. 'You can take your boots to my cousin the cobbler, and he will mend them well for five shillings to-night. Then you can wear them to-morrow.'

'But I don't want to spend my . . . ' began Bossy. He didn't finish. Mr Put-Em-Right told him he didn't know what was good for him. He said he knew better than Bossy. He told him he was only a silly young boy, without an idea in his head. He was altogether most annoying and unpleasant.

'Bossy old fellow!' thought Bossy, driving in the pea-sticks with quite a lot of bad temper. 'I can't get a word in!'

Mr Put-Em-Right found fault with the way Bossy did the strawberry bed. He said he hadn't thinned the lettuces properly. 'Did you water them first so that the thinnings would come up easily? Did you pull out the tiny ones instead of the well-grown ones? No – you didn't. You're a stupid, foolish boy who doesn't use what few brains he's got! Pull up your stockings, boy. Put your tie straight. Smooth down that hair of yours! Tie up that left shoe! You want taking in hand. Well, I'll see what I can do this week!'

Poor Bossy! What a time he had! Mr Put-Em-Right found fault with him every hour of the day. He bossed him all the time. He made him do things his way and not Bossy's way. He kept telling Bossy that everything he did could be done better. He even told Bossy how to spend his five shillings each evening, and what was more, saw that he did it!

So his first day's money went on having his old boots mended. His second day's money went on buying a birthday present for his mother. He happened to mention to Mr Put-Em-Right that his mother was having a birthday, and the old man at once said that he must certainly spend his next five shillings on her.

'Well – I thought I would spend two shillings,' said Bossy, in alarm. Mr Put-Em-Right wouldn't hear of it. 'Such meanness!' he said. 'A nice mother like that and you can't even spend five shillings on her when you've got it. Now you come with me, and we'll go to my friend the jeweller's and see if he has a really nice brooch for five shillings.'

And off he went with Bossy that evening and insisted that he bought a pretty brooch with M in the middle for Mother.

The next five shillings went on getting the

panes of glass mended in the cucumber frame. Bossy had dropped a spade by accident and it had fallen on the frame, cracking three of the panes. Mr Put-Em-Right had flown into a temper about that. 'You'll spend to-day's five shillings on getting that frame mended!' he yelled. 'Careless boy! Stupid boy! Wish I had my old garden-boy back.'

'Was he so good?' asked poor Bossy, who was now beginning to feel that he wasn't so wonderful after all as he had always thought himself to be.

'He's a better boy than you will ever be, because he doesn't think he knows everything, as you do!' said the old man. 'You think you could run this garden yourself, don't you; you think you know better than I do; you think you're a marvellous chap who ought to get his own way all the time! Well, you're not. You're a silly, bossy little fellow who wants a good lesson. And I'll see you get it this week.'

He did. Bossy couldn't seem to do a thing right. He was bossed here, there and all over the place. Many times he thought of throwing down the tools and walking out – but he was afraid of the sharp-tongued Mr Put-Em-Right, so he didn't. He fell silent and, looking gloomy and cross, he tried to do exactly as he was told.

Mr Put-Em-Right spent his next five shillings

for him, as he had done the others, and would not listen to Bossy when he objected. No, off he marched with him, and the money was spent in the way Mr Put-Em-Right suggested, and not in the way that poor Bossy had planned. He could see that he wasn't going to buy the bicycle bell and pump after all!

On the last day the old man paid him his last five shillings. 'There you are,' he said. 'Spend it how you like.'

Bossy stared at him in surprise. He had quite expected Mr Put-Em-Right to tell him how to spend it. The old man laughed out loud.

'You think I'm a horrid, bossy, grumbling old man, don't you?' he said. 'Well, I'm not. You ask Alfred, my gardener, if I am or not. I've just been giving you a lesson, that's all!'

'What do you mean?' said Bossy, in amazement.

'Well, I know your nickname is "Bossy,"' said Mr Put-Em-Right, with a grin, 'and I've heard you bossing all your friends and putting them right, and telling them to do things *your* way, and not theirs. So when you came after this job I thought I'd show you how it felt to be bossed by somebody older and bigger than you. How did you like it?'

'Not at all,' said Bossy, very red in the face. 'I didn't like you either.'

'Of course you didn't,' said Mr Put-Em-Right. 'Nobody likes bossy people. I hate them myself. Well – you can keep your last five shillings and spend it how you like – you deserve to because you stuck at the job so well. There's good stuff in you, Bossy, if you use it the right way. What about trying?'

'Right, sir,' said Bossy, still very red. 'Er – thank you, sir. Good day, sir.'

He went off on his bicycle, thinking very hard.

Did the other children hate him as much as he had hated old Mr Put-Em-Right? Had he been as annoying and tiresome as the old man had been to him, always finding fault and wanting things done *his* way and no other? Did they really call him Bossy behind his back?

Bossy didn't buy his bicycle pump and bell. He went to the sweet-shop and bought five shillings' worth of sweets and chocolates! For once in a way he was doing something that the other children would like, instead of doing something *he* wanted to do!

He shouted to his friends: 'Hi! I've finished

my week's job. Come and share in what I've bought with to-day's wages!'

They did. They were pleased. Bossy seemed changed, but they didn't know why. 'It won't last!' said Jack to Harry. 'I bet old Bossy is just showing off because he's earned a bit of money!'

But it did last. It's true he is a leader now – but he isn't bossy. He's very friendly with old Mr Put-Em-Right now, too, and grateful to him for taking the trouble to put *him* right. So there must have been very good stuff in Bossy after all!

What wonderful adventures

WHEN the sailor doll came to the nursery all the toys stared at him, for they had never seen a doll like him before.

He wore a sailor suit, a sailor hat, and a very wide smile. 'Hallo, mates!' he said. 'Ahoy there!'

'What are you?' said the doll in the pink coat.

'A sailor doll,' said the sailor doll.

'Sailors go to sea,' said the teddy bear, who knew quite a lot. 'Have you been to sea?'

The sailor doll hadn't. He didn't even know what the sea looked like. But that didn't worry him.

'Been to sea?' he said. 'Of course I've been to sea! I've been wrecked three times. My, what wonderful adventures I've had!'

The other toys thought he was marvellous to have been to sea and had so many adventures. The pink pig asked him to tell about an adventure.

'Well, I set sail one fine day and ran into a storm, and my ship overturned,' said the sailor doll. 'I was drowning like anything . . .'

'Ooooh,' said the pig, shivering with excitement. 'Go on. Don't stop like that. What happened?'

The sailor doll thought hard. 'Oh, I caught a big fish, tied a bit of string round its neck, jumped up on its back and made it take me home!'

'You're wonderful!' said the baby doll, and the doll in the pink coat nodded her head too. The sailor doll was pleased. It was nice to be thought so marvellous. Nobody in the toy-shop where he had come from had thought him at all wonderful. They had said he talked too much.

Well, after that he was always ready to tell more and more amazing adventures, and the toys listened to him with wide-open eyes and ears.

'One day when my ship was wrecked I was cast on a lonely island where there was nothing but wild men,' said the sailor doll. 'What do you

think I did? I tamed them and taught them to sit up and beg, and then when we were rescued I took them all home with me and sold them to a circus.'

'Did you sell them as wild men or tame men?' asked the doll in the pink coat.

'I've forgotten,' said the sailor doll grandly. 'I wish I had kept one as my servant. You'd have liked him.'

The baby doll didn't think she would, but she didn't say so. She sighed and wished she too could have adventures like the sailor doll. How marvellous to sail off to sea and keep being wrecked and rescued.

The sailor doll behaved very badly, for he told a great many more untruthful stories, and made himself out to be a brave and fearless sailor. The toys thought such a lot of him that he became a kind of king in the nursery. He was soon ordering everyone about, and shouting at them if they were not quick enough.

Then another doll came to the nursery, a wooden skittle, with a gay little head painted at the top. The sailor stared at him.

'You're a skittle, aren't you?' he said. 'Not a doll, just a skittle. Well, you may like to know that I'm head of this nursery.'

'Why are you?' said the skittle.

'Oh, the sailor doll has travelled so far and

had such adventures!' said the doll in the pink coat. 'He's been ship-wrecked . . .'

'And rode home on a fish . . .' said the bear.

'And he's rescued ever so many people from drowning,' said the baby doll. 'Oh, he's *so* brave!'

'How do you know all this?' said the skittle, looking at the sailor doll.

'Well, the sailor has told us, of course,' said the pink pig. 'He's simply marvellous! We're lucky to have him in our nursery with us.'

'You'd better stand in that corner over there,' said the sailor doll to the skittle, pointing to a

very dark corner of the toy cupboard. 'I always tell everyone where they are to live. That can be *your* corner.'

'I'd rather have this one, thank you,' said the skittle, and stood in the place that belonged to the sailor doll himself. He was very angry and tried to push the skittle over.

But the skittle didn't mind that a bit. Every time he was knocked over he got up again and his painted face grinned widely. 'I'm made to be knocked over!' he said, and gave the sailor doll a crack on the head. 'Let *me* knock *you* over now!'

But all the toys stood up for their beloved sailor, and the skittle could see he was going to have a bad time if he was rude to him, because it was plain that nobody could be friends with him if so. So he said nothing more, but listened in disgust when he heard the sailor doll telling some of his tall stories.

'I can sail any boat there is! I can even sail a

steamer by myself. I've only got to see someone in the water and I jump in and rescue them. You should just see me swim! I'm faster even than a fish!'

The skittle had to hear all this, and he felt sure the sailor doll was making it all up. 'What a boaster! What a fibber!' he thought. 'But there's nothing I can do to stop him, because all the others admire him so much.'

The skittle was a good fellow. He liked giving a helping hand when he could. He liked a good talk, without any nonsense. He liked a good game, and he didn't mind losing, either, so long as the game had been a good one. The toys would have liked him very much if only the sailor doll hadn't always been saying things against him.

Now one day the toys went out for a walk. It was a fine, windy day, and suddenly the sailor doll's hat blew off. It went bowling down the path towards the pond where the ducks lived.

'Oh! My hat, my fine hat!' shouted the sailor doll. 'Bear, go and fetch it.'

The bear and the baby doll went running after the hat. It bowled on merrily, came to the pond and jumped right in! It floated on the water, and the sailor doll gave a howl of dismay.

'The ducks will get it! Bear, wade in!'

The bear didn't like to. The water looked deep. The skittle spoke in his wooden voice.

'Wade in yourself! Go on – you're a sailor doll, aren't you? Wade in yourself – swim for your own hat!'

The baby doll ran round the pond, got a stick, leaned over the water and tried to get the hat in to shore with the stick. But alas – she over-balanced, and fell splash into the water!

'Save me, save me!' she cried, struggling hard. 'I shall drown, I shall drown!'

Everyone looked at the sailor doll. He could swim, he was brave, he was quite fearless, he had saved heaps of people from drowning – now he would be brave again and jump in and save the baby doll.

But he didn't. 'Go on,' said the bear. 'Jump in or the baby doll will drown.' He gave him a push.

'Don't!' said the sailor doll, turning pale. 'I – I can't swim!'

'Well, fetch the boat from the toy-cupboard, and launch it on the pond and sail to the baby doll!' cried the pink pig. 'Quick, quick!'

'I – I – I c – c – can't sail a boat!' stammered the sailor doll. 'Don't make me try. I should fall in and drown. I can't swim or sail a boat.'

'Then jump in and get the doll,' shouted the skittle, in disgust. 'Do *something*!'

But the sailor doll turned and ran away. Oh, the little boaster, oh, the little coward!

It was the wooden skittle that came to the rescue. He threw himself into the water and landed near the baby doll. 'Catch hold of me now. I'm floating!' he cried. 'Catch hold of me. I'm wood and I shan't sink. Get astride me and waggle your legs in the water, and we'll get to shore all right.'

So the baby doll caught hold of him, got her legs across him, worked them hard, and managed to paddle like that to the bank of the pond, where everyone pulled them in to shore.

'You marvellous skittle!' said the baby doll, and hugged him.

'Wonderful fellow!' said the doll in the pink coat.

'Brave and fearless skittle!' said the pink pig. 'A real hero!'

'Pooh!' said the skittle, drying himself by rolling on the grass. 'Pooh! That's the kind of thing you said to that cowardly sailor doll.'

'Ah – but he only *said* brave things – you *do* them!' said the bear. 'We shan't think anything of him now – you shall be head of the nursery.'

The poor sailor doll hid away when the toys came in. How ashamed he was! He could hardly look the skittle in the face.

'I'm not going to laugh at you,' said the skittle. 'I'm only going to tell you this . . . You've boasted of fine brave deeds, and now that the toys see you can't do even one, they turn up their noses at you. Well, if you want to make them friendly again, just turn to and be decent. Look out for some brave deed to do – and DO IT! Don't hide in a corner and cry.'

'Right!' said the sailor doll, in a humble voice. 'I'll try. I really will.'

So he's looking round for a brave deed to do, but one hasn't come along yet. Do you think he'll do it if he gets the chance? I wonder?

The girl who was afraid of dogs

JENNY was down by the seaside, and she was having a lovely time. She bathed each day, she paddled whenever she wanted to, she dug in the sand and built big castles and she sailed her little boat.

After she had bathed, Mummy made her play ball to get her warm. Mummy threw the ball and Jenny had to catch it. If she didn't catch it, she had to run after it, and that made her nice and warm.

There was a little dog who belonged to some other people on the beach, and he loved a game of ball, too. When he saw Jenny playing ball with her mother, he came up to join in.

But Jenny didn't like dogs. She was afraid of them. Once a dog had jumped up at her, asking her to have a game with him, and she had thought he meant to bite her. So after that she had always run away from dogs, and she wouldn't be friends at all.

'Darling, you can't go all through your life being afraid of dogs!' said Mummy. 'That's silly. You must never pat strange dogs unless they wag their tails at you – but there's no need to scream and run away whenever one comes near you.'

'I don't like dogs. They're simply horrid,' said Jenny. 'They've got nasty red tongues they put out at me, and horrid barky voices, and I don't like them.'

The little dog on the beach was such a friendly little fellow. How he wished Jenny would play ball with him. He belonged to a mistress who was rather old, and never played with him.

So every day he ran up to Jenny after her bathe and begged to play ball with her.

Jenny had a most beautiful new ball. It was big and blue and it bounced very well indeed. She was very proud of it because it was nicer than any ball she had ever had. She even took it to bed with her, so you can guess how much she liked it.

She was very angry with the little dog when he tried to join in the game. Whenever she missed the ball her mother threw to her, it rolled away down the beach and the little dog tore after it, yelping in delight.

Jenny wouldn't go near him. She was afraid of him. She stood still and stamped her bare foot on the sand.

'Naughty dog! Horrid dog! Leave my ball alone! I hate you!'

The little dog fetched the ball and dropped it at her feet, wagging his tail. He was hot and his red tongue hung out of his mouth.

'You're a very rude little dog,' said Jenny. 'Put your tongue in! I don't like you. It's no good wagging your tail at me – I know you'd bite me if I came any nearer.'

The little dog sat down and looked sad. He didn't understand why Jenny spoke to him so unkindly. He was such a friendly little dog, not much more than a puppy, and he did so want to be friends with this little girl. She picked up her ball and took it away.

'I shan't play ball whilst that nasty dog is about,' she told her mother. 'I don't like him.'

But the little dog came nearer, hoping that she would throw the ball again. Jenny glared at him. Then she picked up a handful of stones and threw them at him. Two of them hit him and he yelped with pain.

'Oh Jenny! How cruel and unkind!' said Mummy. 'All he wanted was a game – and you hurt him with stones. Now he is limping because his leg is hurt, and see how he has put his tail

down. He doesn't understand. He is very unhappy.'

The little dog was very sad and puzzled. No one had thrown a stone at him before. Boys and girls don't throw stones at dogs or cats or birds nowadays, unless they are the sort of children that are really bad at heart. And it isn't many children who are bad at heart.

All that day the little dog limped. Sometimes he licked the cut on his leg that the stone had made. Often he looked across at Jenny. He didn't come near her, because now he was afraid of her.

Jenny couldn't help feeling ashamed of herself. All the same she was glad that the little dog kept away. When she saw that he didn't come near her, she took out her ball again and

began to play with it by herself. The little dog
didn't even watch.

Jenny threw the blue ball high into the air. It
fell and she tried to catch it. She missed it and
the ball ran quickly down to the beach. It ran
into the sea. A big wave had just broken and
was going back into the sea – and it took the ball
with it.

'Oh!' yelled Jenny. 'My ball! My blue ball!
The sea has got it!'

'You're not to go in after it!' called her
mother. 'The sea is too rough to-day. Those big
waves would knock you over.'

'But I want my ball,' wailed Jenny, watching
her beautiful blue ball bobbing farther and farther out to sea. 'Oh, my lovely ball!'

She stood there, weeping streams of tears

down her cheeks, for she really was very proud of her ball. Now it was gone for ever. It would be thrown up on some other beach, and some other child would find it and play with it. Jenny sobbed bitterly.

The little dog heard her. He had a soft heart, and he could not bear anyone to be sad. He jumped up and ran to the edge of the sea. He was still limping. He looked at the ball and he looked at Jenny. He knew quite well what was the matter, because he liked that ball himself. It was a fine ball for a game!

He didn't remember that Jenny had been unkind to him, shouted at him and thrown stones at him. He only remembered that it was her ball and that she was unahppy because the sea was taking it away.

And into the water he paddled after that ball! A big wave took him off his feet and rolled him over. But he got himself the right way up again, and found that he could swim. So out into the deep water he swam, farther and farther out, his pink tongue hanging from his mouth, his legs working quickly.

'Oh! The little dog is saving my ball for me, Mummy!' cried Jenny. 'Look, do look! Oh, Mummy, isn't he a good, brave little dog! He's getting my ball!'

'That's the same little dog you treated so

unkindly,' said Mummy. 'What a forgiving little fellow he is!'

'He's got the ball. It's in his mouth! He's got it!' cried Jenny. And so he had. He turned round again and swam for the shore, panting, the ball safely in his mouth. He came into shallow water, paddled through it, ran to Jenny and put the ball down at her feet. Then he shook himself, wagged his tail politely, and ran back to his mistress.

'Well!' said Mummy. 'That dog behaves far better than you do, Jenny! You shouted at him and threw stones at him and made him limp, when all he wanted was a game with you. But instead of letting you lose your ball he fetched it for you and gave it to you, and didn't even stay to be thanked.'

'Oh, Mummy, it was so good of him,' said Jenny, her face very red, because she did feel that her mother was right – the little dog had behaved much better to her than she had behaved to him. 'Oh, Mummy, I feel dreadful now. Can you say you are sorry to a dog? Would he understand?'

'I don't expect he wants you to come near him again,' said Mummy. 'I should think he is far more afraid of you now than you ever were of him.'

'I know what I shall do,' said Jenny, suddenly. 'I shall give him this blue ball, Mummy. I like it very much – but so does he. And perhaps if I give him this ball for his very own he might forgive me for hurting him, and he wouldn't be afraid of little girls any more.'

'Well, it would be a very nice thing to do,' said Mummy, looking pleased. 'I always think that when we have done something wrong, the least we can do is to find out some way to put it right. And that might be just the way, Jenny. But won't you be afraid of going up to him? You know how afraid you are of dogs – very silly of you, really, but still, I can't seem to make you different.'

'I *am* afraid of him, because he's a dog,' said Jenny. 'But, all the same, I'm not going to be a coward now. I'm going to give him my ball.'

So she walked across the beach to where the little dog was lying. He raised his head and looked at her. But he didn't wag his tail. He only kept tail-wags for friends, and he was sure this little girl was no friend.

'Little dog,' said Jenny, kneeling down beside him. 'I'm sorry I hurt you. You can have my ball for your own. Here you are.'

The little dog lay and looked at Jenny. He still didn't wag his tail. He was afraid of her. He wouldn't take the ball.

'Take it,' said Jenny. 'It's yours.'

But the little dog didn't move, except to turn his head away. Jenny was upset. She put the ball down beside the dog and left it there. Then she stretched out her hand very nervously – and patted him! It was the first time in her life that she had ever patted a dog! She liked it. She liked the feel of the rough, warm coat. She patted him again.

'Good dog,' she said. 'Good little dog.' Then she ran back to her mother, feeling very glad. The little dog got to his feet and stared after her. What a funny girl! She had patted him and called him good dog – and, bones and biscuits, she had left her ball beside him! She had given it to him! She was a friend after all!

Joyfully he picked up the ball and sped after Jenny. He wagged his tail so hard that it was difficult to see it. 'Wuff!' he said. 'Play a game, won't you!'

'He's forgiven you,' said Mummy. 'He wants to play with you!'

The little dog dropped the ball for Jenny to throw for him. She threw it and he sped after it and brought it back. She threw it again. Then Mummy threw it for both of them, and they had a race to see who could get it first.

And before the day was out the two of them were very good friends indeed. Jenny was patting him and even tickling him, and the little dog was licking her, and jumping up in delight.

'How silly I was to be afraid of dogs!' thought Jenny, when she went to bed that night. 'Why, I like them very much. I'd even like a puppy for my own!'

The beautiful pattern

ONCE upon a time there was a little boy called Morris. He went to school, and he was very good at all his lessons – except drawing. You should have seen the pictures he drew!

'Well, really, Morris, I don't know if this drawing is meant to be a dustbin, a house, an elephant, or a banana!' his teacher said one day. 'And is this the best pattern you can make for me? Well, I really do think you might have done better than this!'

The children often drew patterns in the drawing-lesson, and coloured the patterns they made. Sometimes they were quite simple ones, like this:

O – O – O – O – O – O – O – O – O – O

or prettier ones like this:

ooo + +ooo + +ooo + +ooo + +ooo + +ooo

They could draw what patterns they liked, and they could use the letters of the alphabet or figures or anything they pleased, so long as they

made a really pretty pattern. It was fun to chalk the patterns.

Poor Morris could never think of a good pattern at all. Once he thought it would be a good thing to do a pattern of aeroplanes, but when he drew them they looked rather like birds with no head and two tails – so it wasn't such a good pattern after all!

One day the teacher gave her children some homework to do at the week-end.

'I want you all to think of a really lovely pattern,' she said – 'the sort of pattern that would look nice on our wallpaper. Now do think of an unusual and beautiful one, draw it out on a sheet of paper, and then colour it.'

Poor Morris! When he got home and sat down with his sheet of paper and a pencil, do you suppose he could think of any pattern at all? Not one!

I expect you could think of plenty, and draw them beautifully – but you are cleverer than Morris.

'It's a shame!' thought Morris, leaning his head on his hand. 'I can do sums well – and I'm always top in history – but I just CAN'T draw!'

'Morris! Whatever are you looking so worried about?' called his mother. 'Don't sit and look so gloomy. Put on your hat and coat and go out into the snow. The sun is shining, and it will do you good to go and play.'

So Morris put on his hat and coat and out he went into the snow. He thought he would go to the little wood nearby. It was a lovely place, because the trees grew very close together and made it rather exciting and mysterious.

Off he went, and into the little wood. And there he saw something he had never seen before. It was a little house made of snow! It had snow walls, a snow chimney, windows made of

little sheets of ice, and no door at all – just an opening.

'What a dear little house!' thought Morris. 'I wonder who made it? Surely no one can live there?'

He went up to the house. He peeped in at the window, but he could see nothing through the ice-panes. He went to the doorway and peeped through the opening.

And inside he saw a long-bearded brownie, very busy papering the snow walls of his house!

'Good gracious!' said Morris. 'Are you really a brownie? I didn't think you lived anywhere except in books. Are you real?'

'Well, what a question to ask anyone!' said the brownie crossly. 'What a funny boy you are! Do you think I'm a dream, or something?'

'Well, you might be,' said Morris. 'I say – what a lovely wall-paper! Where did you get it from?'

'I made it myself,' said the brownie. 'I did the pattern myself too. Do you like it?'

'It's a marvellous pattern,' said Morris, looking at it. 'How did you think of it? I can never think of patterns like this.'

'Oh, I don't think of them,' said the brownie, his green eyes shining as he looked at Morris. 'I just go out and look for them!'

'Look for patterns!' cried Morris. 'Well, *I* wish *I* could do that! I'm always getting into trouble at school because I can't do patterns. Where do you see your patterns when you go to look for them?'

'Well, last summer I made a beautiful pattern of daisy-heads,' said the brownie. 'Quite easy too, it was – just a little round middle with petals all round it. I made a most beautiful wall-paper of that. And another time I went out into the woods and found some green bracken just beginning to grow, and to uncurl its green fingers – and I made a pattern of that too.'

'What lovely things to make patterns from!' said Morris. 'But this wall-paper of yours hasn't daisies or bracken on. It's not a flower-pattern at all. What is it? I'm sure you've made it up.'

'No I haven't,' said the brownie. 'I got this pattern from the snow.'

Morris stared at him in surprise. 'But I've never seen the snow in patterns like that!' he said.

'Ah, that's because you haven't looked carefully enough at the snow-crystals,' said the brownie. 'Each snow-crystal is a little pattern in itself – didn't you know that?'

'No, I didn't,' said Morris. 'I don't even know what you mean.'

'Whatever do they teach you at school?' said the brownie, in astonishment. 'Why, at the brownie school I went to we all learnt about the beauty of snow-crystals. Well, I'll tell you. You've seen snowflakes falling, haven't you?'

Of course,' said Morris. 'They are falling again now.'

'Well, each snowflake is made up of snow-crystals,' said the brownie. 'And now, here is a funny thing – every snow-crystal is different, and yet it is the same in one thing – it is six sided! Shall we go and catch some snowflakes and look at them through my magic glass? Then you will see what I mean.'

So out they went into the wood, where the snow was beginning to fall quite thickly. The little brownie took with him a piece of black velvet, and he caught a snowflake on this. Then he took out a round glass in a frame and made Morris look at the snowflake through the glass – and to the boy's great surprise he saw that the flake was made up of snow-crystals lightly joined together, and every single crystal had six sides to it! Not one of them had four sides or five sides or seven sides – each had six. They were all quite different, but they were very beautiful.

'How perfectly lovely!' said Morris, asto-nished. 'Oh, I do like them! Look – here is one rather like the pattern on your wall-paper! No wonder you managed to get such a pretty pat-tern, brownie – why, there are dozens of diffe-rent patterns for you to use in one snowflake!'

'Yes,' said the brownie. 'I chose one the other

day, and drew it out on my paper. Then I
coloured it. Don't you think it will look sweet on
the walls of my new little snow-house?'

'I do,' said Morris. 'You've given me such a
good idea, brownie! I'm going straight home
now to make a snow-crystal pattern. That's my
homework this week-end. I ought to get top
marks, for I am sure no one else will have such a
lovely pattern as mine!'

'Well, good-bye,' said the brownie, going
back into his house. 'I must go on with my
papering. Come back on Monday afternoon and
tell me if you got top marks.'

Morris ran home. He burst into the sitting-
room and told his mother all about the brownie
and his magic glass.

'I wish I had asked him to lend it to me,' he

said. 'Then I could have chosen the prettiest snow-crystal to do – I'm afraid I shan't remember one very well.'

'*I* have a kind of magic glass you can see through,' said his mother. 'It's Daddy's magnifying glass! It makes things look much bigger when you look through it. I'll get it.'

She fetched it, and Morris went outside to catch a snowflake on his coat-sleeve and looked at it through the magnifying glass. Goodness, how lovely the six-sided crystals were! Like stars or flowers, very small and perfect.

'I'll make a pattern just like that one there,' said Morris to himself, and he looked at the crystal very carefully indeed to get it into his memory. Then he went indoors and got his sheet of paper. He drew a row of six-sided crystals, then another and another, till he had a whole page of them. Then he coloured them beautifully and took his pattern to his mother.

'How marvellous!' she cried. 'This is the loveliest pattern you have ever done! How I would like to have it for my wall-paper!'

Well, as you can guess, Morris got top marks for it, and the teacher pinned the pattern up on the wall for everyone to see. Morris could hardly wait for the afternoon to come, because he so badly wanted to tell the brownie that he had done a beautiful snow-crystal and got top marks!

He looked out of the window. The sun was shining brightly and felt quite hot on his hand.

Morris rushed off to the wood as soon as he could – but oh, what a disappointment! The sun had melted the snow, and there was no little snow-house to be seen! There was only a wet pile of paper on which Morris could just see the pattern the brownie had made.

'His wall-paper!' thought Morris. 'Poor little brownie! His house didn't last long. Well – he did me a good turn, no doubt about that! I shall know where to get my patterns from now – I shall look about in the fields and woods for them!'

Would you like to make a pattern of a six-sided snow-crystals? Well, catch a snowflake on something dark and look at it through a magnifying glass! You will see what Morris and the brownie saw – dainty six-sided crystals, all different, and all beautiful!

A tin of yellow polish

EVERYONE would have liked Dame Round-Face very much if only she hadn't been such a borrower. She didn't borrow money – she borrowed things like brooms, lawn-mowers, a drop of milk, a pinch of tea.

And she hardly ever paid for what she borrowed, or gave anything back in return.

The people in Snowdrop Village were generous and kind, and they didn't mind lending anything, but they did get tired of seeing Dame Round-Face popping her head in at their kitchen doors and hearing her say:

'*Have* you got a bit of soap you could lend me? I've run out of mine, and the shops are shut and I simply *must* finish my washing!'

If no one was in when Dame Round-Face called, she would just go in and help herself to what she wanted, and that made people very cross.

'What are we to do about it?' they said to one another. 'We can't let Dame Round-Face go on behaving like this. It's bad for her, and makes us feel very cross.'

But they couldn't do anything about it because Dame Round-Face didn't take any notice of them when they spoke to her about her bad habit.

'Oh, I'll pay it back all right,' she would say, but she hardly ever did.

Now one day she wanted some polish to rub up her kitchen taps and her door-handles. She had none in her tin. It was quite empty! What a nuisance!

'Never mind – I'll borrow some from Mother

Twinkle,' thought Dame Round-Face, and off she went. But Mother Twinkle was out. Dame Round-Face tried the kitchen-door. It opened.

'Good!' thought Dame Round-Face. 'I'll just pop in, get Mother Twinkle's polish, and slip back with it. She won't mind, I'm sure!'

She opened the cupboard door, and looked on the shelves, to see where Mother Twinkle kept her polish, and suddenly her eye caught sight of a tall, thin tin, bright yellow in colour. Tied round the neck of the tin was a magic duster! Dame Round-Face knew it was a magic one, because it changed colour as she looked at it, a thing that magic dusters always do.

'My!' thought the old lady. 'Now this *is* a bit of luck! Magic yellow polish – and a magic duster to polish with! My word!'

It certainly was a bit of luck. The duster was so full of magic that it was quite well able to work by itself, once the polish was tipped out of the tin on to it. It would whisk off to the nearest tap or door-handle and polish away like anything. Dame Round-Face wouldn't need to rub at all – the duster would do it all!

She ran back to her own cottage with the tin and the duster, feeling very pleased. She tipped out some of the yellow polish on to the duster, and then shook it out into the air. It flew off by itself at once, and settled on to the taps over the sink.

'Look at it polishing them!' said Dame Round-Face in delight. 'My goodness me, those taps of mine will shine like the sun!'

They did. They shone so brightly that they seemed like lanterns in the dark corner over the sink. The duster whisked itself about a little and then flew to the door-handles. It began to polish away hard.

'You do the cupboard handles for me too,' said Dame Round-Face, settling herself down in her rocking-chair. 'I'm going to have a little sleep.'

The duster polished all the door-handles and all the cupboard handles. Then it looked around for something else to polish. It saw two brass candlesticks on the mantelpiece and flew off to polish those, first getting itself a little more of the yellow polish out of the tall yellow tin.

When the candlesticks were done the duster couldn't find any more brass to polish. The doors were shut so it couldn't go into any other room to do some polishing there. It felt sad. It went over to Dame Round-Face, but she was fast asleep, and her mouth was wide open. Her face shone red.

The duster bent itself gently forward, made itself a point out of one of its corners, and carefully polished Dame Round-Face's front teeth. Soon they were a bright, shining yellow. The duster was pleased.

It started on Dame Round-Face's nose next. It polished it very, very gently so that she might not wake. The duster had never polished any-

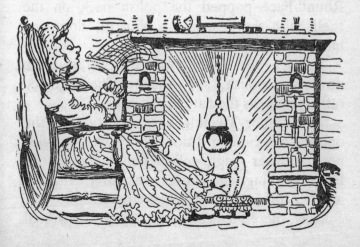

one's face before, and it couldn't help enjoying it.

It polished the old dame's nose till it was as bright yellow as the candlesticks. Then it polished her big ears. Then her cheeks, chin and forehead. It polished away and was quite sorry when it had finished.

It was tired at last and sank beside the tin on the table. After a while Dame Round-Face woke up. She rubbed her eyes, yawned, and looked round the room. How the taps, door-handles and candlesticks shone and twinkled!

'Marvellous!' said Dame Round-Face, very pleased. 'I'd better take the polish and the duster back. If Mother Twinkle isn't home yet, she will never know I've borrowed it!'

Mother Twinkle wasn't home. Dame Round-Face popped the polish back on the shelf, with the duster. She shut the door and hurried home.

'I shan't tell Mother Twinkle I borrowed the duster and polish,' she thought. 'She might be rather cross, as they are magic ones.'

But Mother Twinkle knew as soon as she opened her cupboard door that someone had borrowed her magic yellow polish and duster! For one thing, the duster was dirty, and for another thing the tin was half empty!

'Now, there's a mean trick to play on anyone!'

said Mother Twinkle, crossly. 'To come in while I am out, borrow my things without asking, and put them back without so much as waiting to say thank you! I guess it was old Dame Round-Face! I wish I could punish her. But she is sure to say she didn't borrow anything.'

But Mother Twinkle didn't need to punish Dame Round-Face! She was being dreadfully punished, because of the shining yellow polish on her face and ears! When she went out that afternoon, without looking in her mirror first, she couldn't *think* why people stared at her so hard, and then turned away and laughed!

'She's got a yellow nose!' whispered little Jinky and Lobbo.

'Her ears are shining gold!' giggled Pitapat.

'Her teeth are yellow when she smiles!' laughed Clicky the pixie.

Dame Round-Face hurried home to look in the mirror to see what everyone was staring at. There she saw her shining, gleaming yellow face, set with highly polished yellow ears! Oh, how dreadful, how dreadful!

'That tiresome duster must have polished me too!' cried Dame Round-Face. 'Oh my, oh my! Now I must go to Mother Twinkle and ask her to take away this dreadful yellow-spell.'

How Mother Twinkle laughed when she saw the shining, round, yellow face appearing round her kitchen door.

'Oh, Mother Twinkle, please take away the yellow-spell!' begged Dame Round-Face. 'I simply can't bear it. Everyone is laughing at me.'

'You deserve it,' said Mother Twinkle, beginning to laugh again herself. 'I shan't take the spell away. Keep it on your face to remind you not to borrow! It will wear away gradually as you wash each morning and night.

'And listen to me – although it will slowly fade, Dame Round-Face, it will become yellower again if you borrow anything!' said Mother Twinkle.

Poor Dame Round-Face! The yellow did slowly go away – but it always comes back again if she forgets and begins to borrow anything.

The lost motor-car

ONCE upon a time, George had a toy motor-car that wound up with a little key. It was a yellow car, just big enough to take a little tin man to drive it, and one passenger, who was usually somebody out of the Noah's Ark.

One day George took the car out into the garden to play with. But it wouldn't run on the grass very well, even when it was fully wound up – so he left it there and went to fetch something else.

Whilst he was in the house it began to rain, and his mother called to him to stop in the nursery until the sun shone again. So George forgot about the toy car, and left it out in the garden all day long.

The rain rained on it. Spiders ran all over it. An earwig thought it would make a nice hiding-place and hid under the bonnet. A large fly crept there too.

George didn't remember that he had left it in the garden. He wanted to play with it in two days' time, and he hunted in his toy-cupboard for it – but of course it wasn't there. So he didn't bother any more, though he was sad not to have the little car, because it really was very nice indeed, and could run at top speed twice round the nursery before it stopped.

The little yellow car lost all its bright paint in the next rain-storm. Red rust began to show here and there. Its key dropped out into the grass. The little tin man at the steering-wheel split in half. One of the wheels came loose – so you can see that the toy car was in a very bad way.

And then one morning two little men with baskets came hurrying by. They were pixies, and not much bigger than your middle finger.

In their baskets were loaves of bread and cakes, for the two men were bakers and sold their goods to the Little Folk.

They suddenly saw the old toy motor-car and went up to it in surprise. 'What is it?' said Biscuit.

'It's a car!' said Rusky, his brother. 'An old toy car! Will it go?'

They pushed it – and it ran along on its four rusty wheels, though one wobbled a good bit, because it was so loose.

'It *does* go!' said Biscuit. 'I wonder who it belongs to.'

'I suppose it belongs to the little tin man at the

wheel,' said Rusky. 'But he has split in half, so he's no use any more. I say, Biscuit – if only *we* could have this car! Think how we could take all our loaves and cakes round in no time! Our baskets are sometimes so heavy to carry, and when it rains they get wet. But if we had a car . . . !'

'Oh, Rusky! Do let's have it!' said Biscuit. 'We'll hurry along and deliver our things to-day, and then we'll come back and see what we can do with the car. It's just falling to pieces there – so we might as well have it for ourselves!'

Well, after about an hour the two little bakers came back. They pushed the car off to their tiny house under the hazel bush, and then they had a good look at it.

'It wants a fine new coat of paint,' said Biscuit.

'It wants the wheel tightened,' said Rusky.

'It's got no key,' said Biscuit. 'How will it go?'

'We'll have to rub the wheels with a bit of Roll-Along Magic,' said Rusky, getting excited.

So they set to work. They took the poor little tin man away from the wheel. They screwed the loose wheel on tightly. And then they bought a tin of bright red paint and gave the whole car a beautiful coat of red.

'I think we'll paint the wheels yellow, not red,' said Biscuit. 'It would look gayer.'

So the wheels were painted yellow. Along the sides of the car the two bakers painted their names in yellow letters on the red – 'Biscuit and Rusky, Pixie Bakers.' When they had finished, the little toy car looked very smart indeed.

'Now for a bit of magic to rub on the wheels!' cried Rusky. So they got a bit of Roll-Along Magic and rubbed it on each of the four yellow wheels. Then in they got and drove the car off for its first spin.

It went at such speed! They tore round the garden-path and back, and all the Little Folk came out in surprise to see them. And next day Biscuit and Rusky piled their bread and their

delicious little cakes into the car, and drove off
to deliver them to all their customers. It didn't
take them nearly as long as usual, and they were
just as pleased as could be!

They even bought a tiny horn for the car that
said 'honk-honk!' whenever a worm or a beetle
ran across their path. And it was this horn that
George heard one day when he was playing out
in the garden near the hazel bush!

He heard the 'honk-honk!' and looked round
to see what could be making the noise. He
suddenly saw the little red and yellow car
rushing along, with Biscuit and Rusky inside,
and he stared in such surprise that at first he
couldn't say a word. Then he called out:

'I say! I say! Who are you? Stop a minute, do!'

The car stopped. Biscuit and Rusky grinned
up at George. He stared down at the car. It
looked like the one he had lost – but this was
red with yellow wheels, and his had been all
yellow.

'That's a dear little car you've got,' he said.
'Where did you get it from?'

'We found it under there,' said Rusky, pointing. 'It belonged to a little tin man, who sat at
the wheel – but he had split in half, so we took
the car for ourselves and painted it brightly. Isn't
it fine?'

'You know, it's *my* car!' said George, remem-

bering the little tin man. 'It really is! I must have left it out in the garden. I'm sure I did!'

Biscuit and Rusky stared up at him in dismay. 'Oh dear! Is it really your car? We do love it so – and you can't think how useful it is to us, because we use it to deliver our bread and cakes now, instead of carrying them over our shoulders in baskets. But, of course, if it's yours, you must have it back.'

They hopped out of the car, looking very sad and sorrowful. George smiled at them.

'Of course I shan't take it from you! I shouldn't have left it out in the garden. You've made it simply beautiful – and your names are on it too. You keep it. I'm very pleased to give it to you, and I'll often be looking out for you. Do hoot your horn whenever you pass me, will you? Then I'll know you're there.'

'Of course we will!' said the pixies joyfully, climbing back again into the car. 'You *are* kind! It isn't many children who would give up their toys as quickly as that. Thank you very much indeed!'

They drove off down the path, hooting their horn happily. The car was still theirs! They could still go around as 'Biscuit and Rusky, Pixie Bakers,' and make all the earwigs and beetles scurry out of their way, when they hooted their horn.

Sometimes George finds a little bag on the garden seat, full of tiny sugar-cakes. You can guess where they come from, can't you? They are a little gift from Biscuit and Rusky, and are the most delicious cakes in the world.

You would be surprised at the number of children who peep over the hedge that runs at the bottom of George's garden. They listen for a little 'honk-honk!' and hope that they will see a tiny car rush along with 'Biscuit and Rusky, Pixie Bakers' painted down each side. I guess you'd like to peep over the hedge too!

The strange butterfly

THERE was once a man who collected butterflies. He used to go out into the country with a net and look for any butterfly he still hadn't got in his collection, and try to catch it in his net.

Then he would pop the butterfly into his poison-pot. It would go to sleep there and never wake up again. Then the butterfly-man would take it out, spread its wings out to show them properly, and put it into his butterfly box, stuck on a pin.

One day he went out with his net to look for butterflies. He could only see cabbage whites, red admirals, peacocks – butterflies he knew very well, and had already got.

'This is not going to be my lucky day,' he said to himself. And then quite suddenly he saw a most beautiful butterfly sitting on a flower. It had blue and silver wings with red spots, and quite a big body.

'Never seen one like *that* before!' said the man to himself, and he crept up behind it very, very softly and very, very slowly. He lifted his net – and then suddenly he brought it down, crash – and the beautiful butterfly was caught.

It began to make a noise. It squeaked in a high voice, it fluttered in fright round the big net, it tried its very hardest to get out.

The butterfly-man put his hand into the net to get out his prize. And, to his great surprise, the butterfly bit him on the finger! Bit him very hard, too, so that he cried out in pain, took his hand out of the net, and looked at his bleeding finger.

A little girl came up and looked at the man in surprise. 'What's the matter?' she said. 'Have you hurt yourself?'

'This butterfly bit me,' said the man.

'Butterflies don't bite,' said the little girl. 'They have no teeth. All they have is a sort of tongue they can unroll and dip into flowers to get the honey.'

'Now don't try to teach me anything about butterflies!' said the man, crossly. 'I have collected them all my life. And this one certainly bit me.'

The little girl saw that the butterfly in the net was beginning to flutter again. It called out in a tiny squeak of a voice.

'Let me out! Save me, save me!'

'Good gracious! The butterfly is speaking,' said the little girl. 'I heard it.'

'Don't be silly,' said the man. 'It squeaked, that's all. Some caterpillars and butterflies do squeak.'

'This one talked,' said the little girl. She looked into the net quickly, and then she gave a loud cry.

'You've caught a fairy! It's a fairy, not a butterfly!'

'There aren't such things as fairies,' said the man. 'You really are a silly little girl. Caught a fairy indeed! I don't believe in fairies and never did.'

'Well, you'll never be able to see one, then,' said the little girl. 'That's why you can't see that

this butterfly isn't a butterfly, but a real, live, beautiful fairy. Let her go, please.'

'Certainly not!' said the man. 'It is going to be put into my poison-pot.'

'What – to be killed?' said the little girl in horror. 'Oh, no, no! You mustn't kill a fairy. It's horrid enough to have to kill butterflies, but it would be wicked to kill a fairy. I'll set her free.'

The man grabbed the fairy from the net, opened his poison-pot, and popped the fairy inside. There was just room for her. He put the lid on – and there was the fairy inside the poison-pot, breathing the poisoned air there.

The little girl began to cry, but she couldn't do anything. The man set off again with his butterfly net, without even saying goodbye to her.

'I'd better follow him and see what happens to that poor little fairy!' said the little girl. So she did. And, very soon, the man sat down, leaned his head against the trunk of a tree, and fell fast asleep.

'Now's my chance!' thought the little girl, and she crept up to where the man had put the poison-pot. She took it and opened it.

The poor little fairy was fast asleep inside. The little girl was frightened.

'Perhaps she will never wake up again,' she thought. 'Oh dear! I'll put her here in the shade of this big leaf, and fan her a little.'

So she did – and to her great delight the tiny

fairy stirred at last, stretched her lovely silver and blue wings, and sat up.

'I feel ill,' she said.

'There's a dewdrop above your head; drink it,' said the little girl, in a gentle voice. The fairy sipped from the silver dewdrop, and felt better. She flew up to the little girl's lap.

'You saved me from that horrid man, didn't you?' she said. 'You are a dear little girl! I'll give you three wishes! You can wish them whenever you like!'

She flew off on her pretty wings. The little girl looked at the sleeping man. She saw that he had a small gold watch in his waistcoat pocket, and she giggled. She gently took out the ticking watch, popped it into the poison-pot and put the lid on.

'What a surprise he'll get when he finds his beautiful butterfly is gone, and his watch is in the pot instead!' she thought. 'Oh dear, how I do wish that every boy and girl could hear about this funny adventure of mine!'

Well, that was a wish, wasn't it? And, like all magic wishes, it has come true. I'd like to wish a wish, too – I wish I could have seen the butterfly-man's face when he opened the pot to show his friends the strange butterfly, and found his gold watch there instead!

Do hurry up, Dinah!

ONCE upon a time there was a little girl called Dinah. She was pretty and had nice manners, and she was kind and generous.

But, OH, how slow she was!

You should just have seen her dressing in the morning. She took about five minutes finding a stocking. Then she took another five minutes putting it on. Then she spent another five minutes taking it off because it was inside out. By the time she was dressed and downstairs everyone else had finished breakfast.

At breakfast-time she was just as slow. You really would have laughed to see her eating her porridge. First she sat staring at her plate. Then she put the sugar on very, very slowly and very, very carefully. Then she put on her milk. She stirred the porridge slowly round and round and round, and then she began to eat it.

She took quite half an hour to eat it, so she was always late for school. And, dear me, when she did get to school what a time she took taking off her coat and hat. What a time she was getting out her pencil and rubber and book! By the time that Dinah was ready to begin her work the lesson was finished.

She had two names. One was Slow-coach, which her mother called her, and the other was Tortoise, which her teacher called her.

'Dinah, you should have been born a tortoise!' the teacher used to say. 'You really should. You would have been quite happy as a slow old tortoise!'

'Well,' said Dinah, 'I wish I lived in Tortoise-town, wherever it is! I hate people always saying "Do hurry up, Dinah; do hurry up, Dinah!" I'd *like* to live with tortoises. I'm sure they wouldn't keep hustling and bustling me like everyone else does.'

Now it so happened that the wind changed at the very moment that Dinah said this. You know that many queer things are said to happen when the wind changes, don't you? Well, sometimes a wish will come true at the exact change of the wind – and that's what happened to Dinah!

Her wish came true. She suddenly found that everything round her went quite black, and she put out her hand to steady herself, for she felt giddy.

She caught hold of something and held on to it tightly. The blackness gradually faded, and Dinah blinked her eyes. She looked round, expecting to see the school-room and all the boys and girls sitting down doing writing.

But she didn't see that. She saw something most strange and peculiar – so peculiar that the little girl blinked her eyes in astonishment.

She was in a little village street! The sun shone down overhead, and around Dinah were funny little houses, with oval doors, instead of oblong ones like ours.

She was holding on to something that was beginning to get very angry. 'Let go!' said a slow, deep voice. 'What's the matter? Let go, I say! Do you want to pull my shell off my back!'

Then, to Dinah's enormous surprise, she saw that she was holding tightly on to a tortoise as big as herself! He was standing on his hind legs, and he wore a blue coat, short yellow trousers, and a blue hat on his funny little wrinkled head.

Dinah stared at him in amazement. 'Who are you?' she asked.

'I'm Mr Crawl,' said the tortoise. 'Will you leave go, please?'

Dinah let go. She was so surprised and puzzled at finding herself in a strange village all of a sudden with a tortoise walking by, that she could hardly say a word. But at last she spoke again.

'Where am I?' she asked.

'In Tortoise-town,' said the tortoise. 'Dear me, *I* know you! You're the little girl that is called Tortoise at school, aren't you? You wanted to come here, didn't you – and here you are! Well, well – you'd better come home with me and my wife will look after you. Come along.'

'I want to go home,' said Dinah.

'You can't,' said Mr Crawl. 'Here you are and here you'll stay. No doubt about that. You should be pleased that your wish came true. Dear, dear, don't go so quickly. I can't possibly keep up with you!'

Dinah wasn't really going quickly. She always walked very slowly indeed – but the old tortoise shuffled along at the rate of about an inch a minute!

'Do hurry up!' said Dinah at last. 'I can't walk as slowly as this. I really can't.'

'My dear child, you were called Tortoise at school, so you must be very, very slow,' said Mr Crawl. 'Now, here we are at last. There's Mrs Crawl at the door.'

It was all very astonishing to Dinah. She had passed many tortoises in the road, some big, some small, all wearing clothes, and talking slowly to one another in their queer deep voices. Even the boy and girl tortoises walked very slowly indeed. Not one of them ran!

Mrs Crawl came slowly to meet Dinah and Mr Crawl. She did not look at all astonished to see Dinah.

'This little girl has come to live in Tortoise-town,' said Mr Crawl. 'She needs somewhere to live, so I have brought her home.'

'Welcome!' said Mrs Crawl, and patted Dinah on the back with a clawed foot. 'I expect you are hungry, aren't you? We will soon have dinner! Can you smell it cooking?'

Dinah could and it smelt delicious. 'Sit down and I will get dinner,' said Mrs Crawl. Dinah sat down and watched Mrs Crawl get out a tablecloth.

It took her a long time to open the drawer. It took her even longer to shake out the cloth. It took her simply ages to lay it on the table!

Then she began to lay the table with knives and forks and spoons. It took her over half an hour to do this, and poor Dinah began to get more and more hungry.

'Let *me* put out the plates and glasses,' she said impatiently, and jumped up. She bustled round the table, putting the things here and there. Mrs Crawl looked at her crossly.

'Now for goodness' sake don't go rushing about like that! It's bad for tortoises! It's no good getting out of breath and red in the face.'

'I'm not a tortoise,' said Dinah.

'Well, you soon will be when you have lived here a little while,' said Mr Crawl, who had spent all this time taking off one boot and putting on one slipper. 'You'll see – your hair will fall off and you'll be bald like us – and your neck will get wrinkled – and you'll grow a fine hard shell.'

Dinah stared at him in dismay. 'I don't want to grow into a tortoise!' she said. 'I think you look awful.'

Mr and Mrs Crawl gazed at Dinah in great annoyance. 'Rude little girl,' said Mrs Crawl. 'Go and wash your hands – Mr Crawl will go and wash his first and show you where to run the water.'

It took five minutes for Mr Crawl to walk to the wash-place. It took him ten minutes to wash and dry himself, and by that time Mrs Crawl had actually got the dinner on the table. Dinah was so hungry that she washed her hands more quickly than she had ever washed them in her life before!

Oh dear – *what* a long time Mr and Mrs Crawl took over their soup. Dinah finished hers long before they were half-way through, and then had to sit and wait, feeling dreadfully hungry, whilst they finished. She fidgeted, and the two tortoises were cross.

'What an impatient child! Don't fidget so! Learn to be slower, for goodness' sake! You wanted to come and live with us, didn't you? Well, be patient and slow and careful.'

Dinner wasn't finished till four o'clock.

'Almost tea-time!' thought Dinah. 'This is simply dreadful. I know now how horrid it must be for everyone when I am slow at home or at school. They must feel as annoyed and impatient as I do now.'

'I'll take you out for a walk when I'm ready,' said Mrs Crawl. 'There's a circus on in the market-place, which perhaps you would like to see.'

'Oh yes, I would!' cried Dinah. 'Oh, do hurry up, Mrs Crawl. I'm sure that by the time you've got your bonnet on, and your shawl, the circus will have gone!'

'Nobody ever says "Do hurry up!" in Tortoise-town,' said Mrs Crawl, shocked. 'We all take our own time over everything. It's good to be slow. We never run, we never do anything quickly at all. You must learn to be much, much slower, dear child.'

It was six o'clock by the time that Mrs Crawl had got on her bonnet, changed her shoes and put on a nice shawl. Dinah thought that she had never in her life seen anyone so slow. Sometimes Mrs Crawl would stop what she was doing, and sit and stare into the air for quite a long time.

'Don't dream!' cried Dinah. 'Do hurry up!' And then she remembered how very, very often people had cried out the same thing to her, crossly and impatiently. 'What a tiresome nuisance I must have been!' she thought. 'Oh dear – I didn't like hurrying up, but I hate even worse this having to be *so* slow!'

The circus was just closing down when they reached it. The roundabout was starting for the very last time. Dinah could have cried with disappointment. She got on to a horse, and the roundabout began to play. It turned round very slowly indeed.

Dinah looked at all the creepy-crawly tortoises standing about, looking so solemn and slow, and she couldn't bear them.

'Oh, I wish I was back home!' she cried. 'I wish I was. I'd never be slow again, never!'

The roundabout horse that she was riding suddenly neighed loudly. Dinah almost fell off in surprise. It turned its head and looked at her.

'I'm a wishing-horse!' it said. 'Didn't you know? Be careful what you wish!'

The roundabout went faster. It went very fast. Then it slowed down and stopped – and hey presto, what a surprise! Dinah was no longer in Tortoise-town, but in a field at the bottom of her own garden! She knew it at once. She jumped off the horse and ran to the gate in her own garden wall. She looked back at the round-about – and it slowly faded like smoke, and then it wasn't there any more.

Dinah tore up the garden path. She rushed up the stairs to the nursery. Her mother was there, and stared in amazement. She had never seen Dinah hurry herself before!

'What's happened to you?' she asked. 'You're really being quick for once.'

'I've been to Tortoise-town!' said Dinah. 'And now I'm back again, hurrah! I'll never be a

slow-coach or a tortoise again, never, never, never!'

She probably won't. Is there anyone you know that ought to go to Tortoise-town? Not you, I hope!

A present for Granny

'It's Granny's birthday to-morrow,' said Cousin Betty to George.

'Oh dear!' said George. 'So it is. And I had forgotten all about it. I haven't even a penny in my money-box to buy her a present.'

'I've got sixpence,' said Cousin Betty. 'I've been saving up. I shall buy Granny two packets of nice grey hairpins. She will like those. She won't think much of *you*, George, if you don't give her a present.'

'I did have lots of money before I came away to the seaside,' said George, 'but I spent it all on this big spade and a fishing-net. Bother! I wish Mummy had reminded me that it was Granny's birthday.'

'I did,' said Mummy, from her deck-chair. 'But I expect you forgot in all the excitement of coming to the seaside.'

George was worried. He liked Granny, and he liked remembering people's birthdays. He didn't want Cousin Betty to give Granny a present if he didn't. But he knew she would. She always liked

to remember things that other people forgot. She would be pleased to think that she would be the only grandchild to give Granny something.

'Well, I simply must give her a present,' thought George, digging hard in the sand. 'I wonder if there is anything she would like that doesn't cost money?'

He wondered if there were any nice shells on the shore. Perhaps if there were he could bore a tiny hole in each and thread them together to make a necklace. So he looked. But there were no pretty shells at all, only great big ones, half-broken.

Then he found a five-fingered starfish lying on the sand. It was the first time George had ever found a starfish, and he thought it must be very rare and quite valuable. He put it into his pail and carried it proudly to Mummy.

'Look what I've got for Granny,' he said. 'A very rare starfish. That would be a lovely present for her, wouldn't it, Mummy?'

'No,' said Mummy. 'I'm

afraid Granny doesn't like starfish, darling. And certainly it wouldn't like being a birthday present.'

'Oh Mummy – do let me give it to Granny,' begged George. 'I'm sure she would like it. I can't find any nice shells to thread.'

'Isn't he silly?' said Cousin Betty to Mummy. 'Fancy thinking of giving a stupid, ugly starfish for a birthday present. I think Cousin George is a baby. He's a baby for not remembering about Granny's birthday and saving up for it and he's a baby for thinking she would like a silly starfish for a present.'

George nearly threw the poor starfish at Cousin Betty, he felt so angry with her. But he didn't, because he knew the starfish wouldn't like it. He went very red, and ran down the beach with his pail. He emptied the starfish into a pool of water.

Then, in the pool, he saw what he thought were beautiful sea-flowers. They were sea anemonies, red and green, whose feelers waved about in the water like flower-petals. They were really sea-animals, not sea-flowers, but George didn't know that.

'Oh! I'll pick these and take them to Granny!' he thought, pleased. 'They are really lovely.'

But they seemed to be stuck hard on to the side of the rock and he couldn't get them off.

Also, when he touched them, they drew in their pretty feeler-like petals and looked like ugly lumps of jelly. It was very disappointing.

Betty came along, and how she laughed when she saw George trying his hardest to pick the anemones.

'Don't tell me you are going to pick a bunch of those and take them to poor Granny!' she cried. 'What a little silly you are! They are not proper flowers, Cousin George, they are queer little sea-animals, all mouth and tummy, with feelers waving round the edge to catch something to eat!'

George really did feel silly then. He couldn't pick off the lumps of jelly – and anyway, they weren't like pretty flowers any more. He glared at Betty.

'You're a horrid girl. Go away. You're always laughing at me. I don't like you.'

He walked off by himself. Then he saw something scuttling quickly along over the sand. George looked at it and saw that it was a small crab – but what a pretty one!

'I've never seen such a dear little crab!' said George. 'Never! It's green and small and it looks so friendly. I do like it.'

He picked up the crab and it seemed to nestle into his hand, curling up its legs under its body. He took it to his mother.

'Mummy! I shall give this to Granny for her birthday. It's the prettiest crab I ever saw in my life, and it's so friendly and tame. Look! It's curled up in my hand. I'm sure Granny would like it for a pet. She said the other day that she hadn't even a cat to pet now. I shall give her this crab.'

'No, darling,' said Mummy. 'It is a dear little crab, I agree. But I am sure Granny would rather not have it. It would soon die. It wouldn't be kind to keep it as a pet.'

Cousin Betty ran up and peered down at the crab. 'Good gracious! You're surely not thinking of giving *that* to Granny, are you? She would *laugh*!'

'She wouldn't,' said George. 'I know she wouldn't. She never laughs at me. Nobody does, except you.'

'Now, don't quarrel,' said Mummy. 'And don't look so disappointed, George. Go and put the poor little crab back on the sand. Granny really won't mind if you haven't a present for her.'

George ran down to the sand. Betty ran after him. 'Let's play with the crab. Let's pretend he's a spider, and our hands are birds going after him to eat him.'

'No,' said George. 'That would frighten him. He's such a dear little crab.'

Betty made a grab at the crab. George pushed her away and set the tiny thing on the wet sand. Betty pounced on him, but he scrabbled hard with his legs, and began to sink down into the sand and disappear. Soon he was gone.

'You can't get him now,' said George, pleased. 'Didn't he disappear quickly?'

George dug about in the wet sand with his fingers, trying to feel if the crab was anywhere about. But he wasn't. George suddenly felt something round and hard down in the wet sand, and pulled it up with his finger and thumb. It was all sandy. George dipped it into a pool of water and cleaned it – and, goodness gracious me, it was a shilling!

'A whole shilling!' said George, in surprise and delight. 'Mummy, Mummy, look what I've found, just where the little crab sank down – a shilling, a silver shilling!'

Mummy was very surprised. She sent George to ask the other children on the beach if they had dropped any money, but they hadn't. Mummy said it might even have been lost the year before, and stayed buried in the sand till George found it.

'You are very lucky,' she said. 'You may keep the shilling for yourself as we don't know who lost it. We can always give a shilling to anyone if we do hear it has been lost.'

'Oh, Mummy, now I can buy a present for Granny!' said George, beaming all over his round face. 'A nice present, too. Oh, I *am* glad I put the little crab back into the sand. He found the shilling for me!'

George went off to the shops, and what do you think he found in one of them marked at a shilling? He found a small brooch in the shape of a tiny green crab! It really was very quaint and pretty. He bought it for his Granny.

'It's a much nicer present than my packets of hairpins,' said Cousin Betty, not at all pleased. 'I wish you had only found sixpence.'

'You're not a very kind little girl, Betty,' said Mummy. 'You have teased George a lot this morning, and he was only trying to find something to please his Granny. I should have thought a lot more of you if you had helped him, or had even offered to let him have one of your packets of hairpins to give Granny.'

Then it was Betty's turn to go red. Mummy didn't often speak to her little niece like that, and Betty felt sad.

Granny loved the little crab-brooch, and listened in surprise to George's story of how he found a crab which had shown him the lost shilling.

'Well, I must say I like a crab-brooch better than a live crab!' said Granny, kissing George. 'Thank you for a lovely present, George. It was nice of you to spend the whole shilling on me.'

She liked Betty's hairpins, too, but both George and Betty knew the little crab-brooch was much the nicer present.

'I shan't tease you any more, George,' said Cousin Betty. 'It was mean of me. It serves me right that you should have got such a lovely present for Granny.'

'Oh, don't worry about that,' said George. 'The very next shilling I find I'll spend on *you*, Betty! I promise you that.'

He hasn't found another shilling yet, but you

should just see how he digs down after any crab that sinks into the sand! He says he knows another crab will find him a shilling. I hope I hear if it does.

THE ENID BLYTON TRUST
FOR CHILDREN

We hope you have enjoyed the adventures of the children in this book. Please think for a moment about those children who are too ill to do the exciting things you and your friends do.

Help them by sending a donation, large or small, to the ENID BLYTON TRUST FOR CHILDREN. The trust will use all your gifts to help children who are sick or handicapped and need to be made happy and comfortable.

Please send your postal orders or cheques to:

> The Enid Blyton Trust For Children,
> Lee House,
> London Wall,
> London EC2Y 5AS

Thank you very much for your help.